E Turner, Ann
T Heron Street

DATE DUE			
DE 02 '91			
DE 23 '91	2 0		
JA 06 '92	1 0 0		
OC1 7 '94			
NO0 7 '96			
MR 24 '97			
3	MR 1 2 '98		

HERON STREET

Library of Congress Cataloging-in-Publication Data
Turner, Ann Warren.
    Heron street/by Ann Turner; illustrations by Lisa Desimini. — 1st ed.
      p.   cm.
    "A Charlotte Zolotow book."
    Summary: Exploration of a marsh near the sea that used to be home for
many animals and birds, but that men have slowly destroyed and turned
into a noisy city.
    ISBN 0-06-026184-6 : $.
    ISBN 0-06-026185-4 (lib. bdg.) : $.
    [1. Man—Influence on nature—Fiction.]   I. Desimini, Lisa, ill.   II. Title
PZ7.T8535He 1989   87-24948
[E]—dc19   CIP
                                                                    AC

Typography by Al Cetta
1 2 3 4 5 6 7 8 9 10
First Edition

For Patty, with love

AT

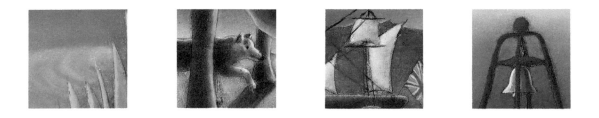

To Mom, Dad, Natalie, and Jerry

LD

Heron Street

by Ann Turner

Paintings by Lisa Desimini

Harper & Row, Publishers

In the beginning they lived in a marsh by the sea—
herons, ducks, geese, raccoons.
Rattlesnakes and wolves lived
along its drier edge.

"Sqwonk-honk, chee-hiss, aroooo!"

And the wind in the tall grass

sang, "Shhh-hello, hsss-hello."

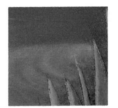

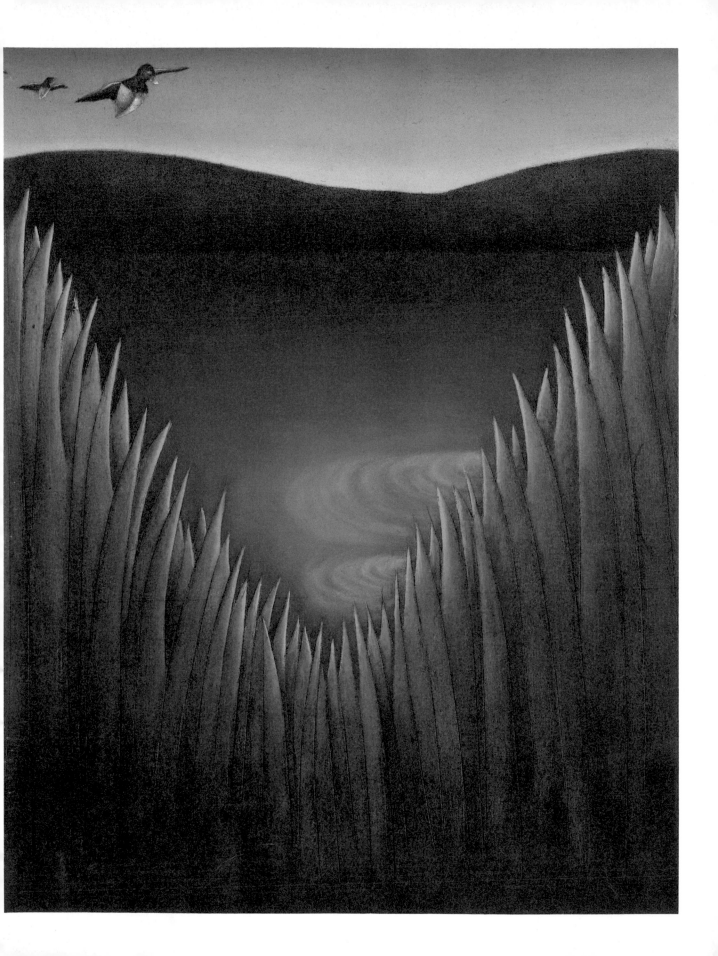

Men came from across the sea,

and women and children,

to build by the marsh and fish in the bay.

"Ca-thunk!" They built logs into houses.

"Moooo." Cows grazed and made milk.

"Clunk-a-chunk." The butter churns started.

And always the wind blew through the grass,

"Shhh-hello, hsss-hello."

Children and pigs and families spread beside the marsh.

Bells called people to church, "Bong-a-dong, dong."

In school, children chanted, "In Adam's fall, we sinned all."

Pigs rooted in the dirt. "Scrunch-snort!"

But the wolves loped away to a land

where there were no churches, or schools, or bells.

The grass still sounded, "Shhh-hello, hsss-hello."

Men came from across the sea and fought
with the settlers by the marsh.

"Barooom!" sang the cannons.

"Crack!" went the rifles,

and the soldiers cried as they fell.

When the British sailed home,

bells rang to celebrate, "Dong-bong, dong-bong,"

and people shouted and waved, "Ray-ooray-ray!"

So many people built near the marsh

that earth was brought to fill it up.

But the animals and birds were leaving,
the geese flapping high overhead. "Honk!"
The herons left their nests. "Sqwonk!"
And most of the grass was cut to make room
for houses. "Hsss-shhh, hsss-shhh."

Gaslights bloomed on the new streets

like flowers, and lit with a "Pop!" at night.

Sometimes a wood house caught fire

and the wagons rushed by,

their bells swinging. "Rang-a-clang, rang-a-clang."

Out at sea, the buoys sang, "Bong-dong, bong-dong."

The small patch of grass that was left

still swayed in the wind. "Shhh-hello, hsss-hello."

On the land where once herons nested,
automobiles chugged down the streets, "Sputter-pop!"
and their horns blew, "A-ooga, a-ooga."

Trolleys sped along the rails. "Ding-bing, ding-bing!"

The patch of grass grew smaller and smaller,

and no one heard the wind saying, "Shhh-hello, hsss-hello."

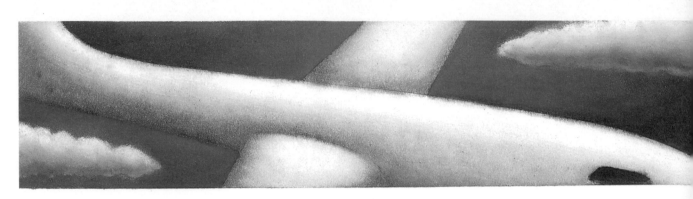

Now airplanes land. "Whine-aroom!"

A car goes round a corner, "Varoom-screech!" and

music sings from a doorway, "Whip-bop-de-be-bop."

Children and dogs and houses bloom

like crowded flowers,

and roller skates sound on tar, "Chirr-whirr."

On a cool fall night, one heron flies low overhead.

It soars over a backyard where a dog bays,

but then it circles and flies higher, its legs

like a long, thin good-bye, calling,

"Sqwonk-sqonk-sqwonk." Below, the small patch of grass answers, "Shhh-hello, hsss-hello."